Enid Blyton's
Bunny and the Pixies

ILLUSTRATED BY JO CAINE

D0320196

A TEMPLAR BOOK

Produced by The Templar Company plc, Pippbrook Mill, London Road, Dorking, Surrey RH4 1JE

Text copyright © *Bunny and the Pixies* 1926-1953 by Darrell Waters Limited
This edition illustration and design copyright © 1995 by The Templar Company plc
Enid Blyton's signature mark is a registered trademark of Darrell Waters Limited

This edition produced for Parragon Book Sevice Ltd, Units 13-17, Avonbridge Trading Estate, Atlantic Road, Avonmouth, Bristol BS11 9QD

This book contains material first published as *Where's My Tail?* in Enid Blyton's Sunny Stories
and Sunny Stories between 1926 and 1953.

Printed and bound in Italy

ISBN 0-75251-436-9

•PARRAGON•

Elizabeth had been having
a lovely picnic with her toys,
but now it was time to
go home.

Off they all went. Teddy, Panda
and Bun, a fat little toy rabbit
with big furry ears.

After Elizabeth had put them back in the playroom, Teddy, Panda and Bun told the other toys all about their picnic. The little clockwork mouse listened – but it wasn't long before he started to giggle.

"*What* is the matter with you, Clockwork Mouse?" said Teddy, at last. "What's so funny?"

"It's Bun," he said, with one of his sudden giggles. "He does look funny, don't you think?"

"Why, what's the matter with him?" said Teddy, surprised. And when Clockwork Mouse told them, the toys gave a cry of astonishment,

for Bunny had lost his tail. It had completely disappeared! Bun screwed his head round and looked at himself. "Oh dear! Oh dearie me! Where's my tail? I must have dropped it."

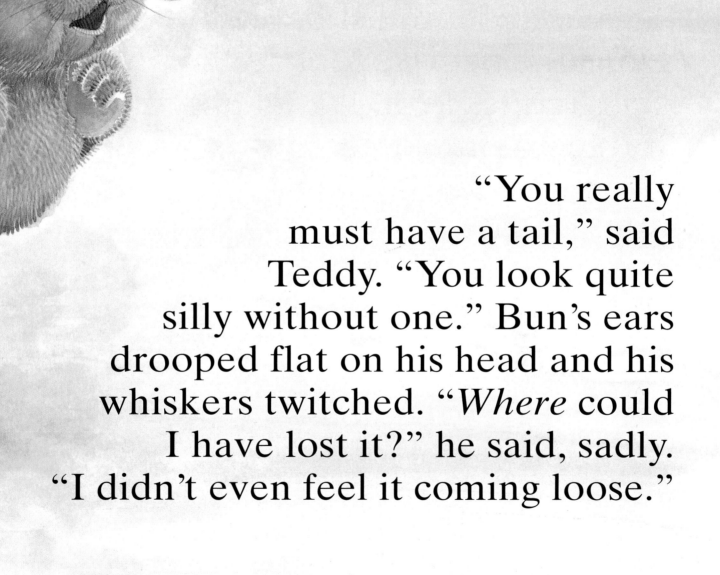

"You really
must have a tail," said
Teddy. "You look quite
silly without one." Bun's ears
drooped flat on his head and his
whiskers twitched. "*Where* could
I have lost it?" he said, sadly.
"I didn't even feel it coming loose."

"Well, you can start by looking along the path we took to the picnic," said Teddy. "You'll probably find it there. Cheer up!"

There didn't seem to be anything else to do but go and look. So Bun set off by himself.

Soon he came to the
woodland path, and looked
very carefully in the grass.
But there was no tail there.

A robin called to him: "Hello, Bun! What are you doing?"

"I'm looking for my tail," said Bun. "Have you seen it?"

"No," said Robin. "But Prickles the Hedgehog might know where it is. He passed this way a few minutes ago. I only hope he hasn't eaten it."

What a dreadful thought! Bun's ears went flat again. He hopped quickly down the path after the hedgehog.

"Prickles!" he called as soon as he saw him in the distance. "Have you seen my tail? I've lost it."

"Very careless of you," said Prickles. "You'll be losing your ears and your whiskers next."

"Don't say that," said Bun. "I'm just asking if you've seen my tail."

"No," said Prickles. "I'll look out for it. Would it be nice to eat?"

"No, certainly not," said Bun. "It might make you ill."

The hedgehog went off to look for something else to eat and Bun hopped on down the path. But he couldn't see his tail anywhere.

Then suddenly he heard somebody singing. Who could it be?

He came to a big oak tree and peeped round it. Beyond lay a tiny dell, surrounded by tall foxgloves, and in the middle of them sat a small pixie. She was rocking a tiny pixie baby in a little silvery cot!

How Bun stared! He had never seen a pixie before. Never! How beautiful she was! And, oh, what a tiny baby! Why, it was as small as the smallest doll in the dolls' house.

Bun crept nearer. He poked his soft little nose between two tall foxglove stems and watched.

The pixie lifted the baby up and put it on her knee. Then she began to tidy the cot. First she shook out a tiny blanket made of cobwebs. Then she smoothed the cot's soft, fluffy mattress.

Bun watched. He suddenly flicked his ears up straight and glared. Yes, he glared! Then he squeaked very angrily indeed, and rushed straight over to the pixie and her baby. She looked up in alarm at the angry rabbit.

"Oh, whatever is the matter?" she said. "You gave me quite a fright." "That's my tail!" said Bun, fiercely, and he pointed with his paw at the fluffy mattress.

"That's *my tail*!
And I want it back right now!"

"Oh, dear!" said the pixie, hushing the baby who had started to cry in a high, tinkling voice. "Is it really your tail? I'm terribly sorry. I found it in the grass over there – and it's such a soft, fluffy little thing, perfect for my baby to lay on. I couldn't possibly guess it was a tail."

"Well, it is," said Bun, looking a little less fierce. "It's mine. How do you suppose I felt without a tail? I felt dreadful. And all the toys laughed at me!"

"I'm so sorry!" said the pixie, and she held Bun's tail out to him. "You must take it back straight away."

Bun held his fluffy tail between his paws. He *was* glad to have it back again. "Why, it smells of honeysuckle," he said in surprise.

"Yes, I hope you don't mind," said the pixie. "I put some special fairy perfume on it to make it nice for Baby. She had such a lovely sleep."

The baby suddenly put out her tiny arms to Bun and caught one of his ears. She pressed it against her rosy cheek, gurgling softly.

"Hold her for a minute," said the pixie. "I want to get something." And to Bun's surprise she put the tiny pixie baby into his furry arms. She had green eyes, as green as the grass, and tiny pointed ears. Bun thought she was the most beautiful little baby he had ever seen!

The pixie came back with a needle and thread – and a big pink silk ribbon. "I'm going to sew your tail on for you," she said. "And I'm going to tie this new pink ribbon round your neck, just to say thank you for being so kind to us."

"I'm sorry I frightened you," said Bun. "I was just so surprised when I saw you using my tail for a mattress. But your baby's so nice that I really don't mind a bit now."

The pixie sewed on the tail. Bun sniffed hard. "I do smell nice!" he said, pleased. "Thank you very much. And, oh – what a fine ribbon for my neck! None of the other toys have a ribbon as fine as this."

The pixie tied it round his neck in a beautiful bow. "There! You look a very smart rabbit indeed. I do hope you'll come back and see us again soon, and bring some of your friends with you next time."

"Oh, yes please,"
said Bun, delighted.
"I will bring Panda and
Teddy too. They would
love to see a pixie baby.
I'm sure they would."
Then Bun looked
up and was surprised

to see that the sky was
as pink as the ribbon
round his neck. The sun
was setting and it was
time for him to go home.

"Well, I must go now. Thank you for finding my tail." And he scampered off, full of excitement. What a dear little baby! How nice and small and cuddly it had felt – and to think that soon he would be able to show her to the other toys! He gave an extra big skip and jump because he felt so happy.

The toys
crowded round
him when he got back.
"You've found your tail!
Who sewed it on for you?
Oh, Bun, you *do* smell nice!"

So Bun told them the whole story, and now the toys are longing to meet the pixie baby themselves. And whenever Bun smells his honeysuckle-scented tail, it reminds him of that tiny pixie baby in the foxglove dell. How I'd love to have seen it, too! Wouldn't you?